GEORGE AND MARTHA BACK IN TOWN

JAMES MARSHALL

Houghton Mifflin Company   Boston

For Rhoda Dyjak

Library of Congress Cataloging in Publication Data

Marshall, James, 1942–
George and Martha back in town.

Summary: Though their friendship is often tested,
George and Martha survive with a sense of humor.
[1. Friendship — Fiction] [2. Hippopotamus — Fiction]
I. Title.
PZ7.M35672Gc   1984   [E]   83-22842

RNF   ISBN   0-395-35386-6
PAP   ISBN   0-395-47946-0

Printed in China

WKT 25 24 23 22 21

FiVE STORiES ABOUT TWO DEAR FRiENDS

STORY NUMBER ONE

THE BOX

Martha noticed a little box
on George's kitchen table.
"Do not open," said the sign.
"I won't," said Martha.
"I'm not the nosy type."
But Martha couldn't take her eyes off
the little box.
She read the sign again.
"Do not open," said the sign.
Martha couldn't stand it.
"One little peek won't hurt," she said.
And she untied the string.

Out jumped George's entire collection of
Mexican jumping beans.
"Oh my stars," said Martha.

It took Martha all afternoon

to round up the Mexican jumping beans.

One yellow one gave her quite a chase.

When George came home
Martha was reading a magazine.
"You seem out of breath," said George.
"You don't think I opened that little box,
do you?" said Martha.
"Of course not," said George.
"I'm not the nosy type," said Martha.

George didn't say a word.

STORY NUMBER TWO
THE HIGH BOARD

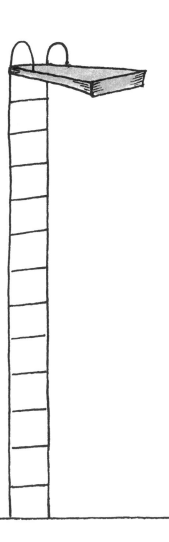

"Today," said George, "I will jump from
   the high board!"

"Don't do it!" cried Martha.

"Everyone will be watching!" said George.

"You'd never catch *me* up there!" said Martha.

"That's because you're a scaredy-cat," said George.

But when George got up on the high board,

he lost his nerve.

"I can't do it," he said.

"And everyone is watching!"

His knees began to shake.

"I'll be right up," said Martha.

Martha climbed up the ladder.

"Now what?" said George.

"I'll go first," said Martha.

And she jumped off.

Martha caused quite a splash.

Everyone was impressed.

And no one noticed how George got down.

"I just didn't feel like it today," said George.

Martha didn't say a word.

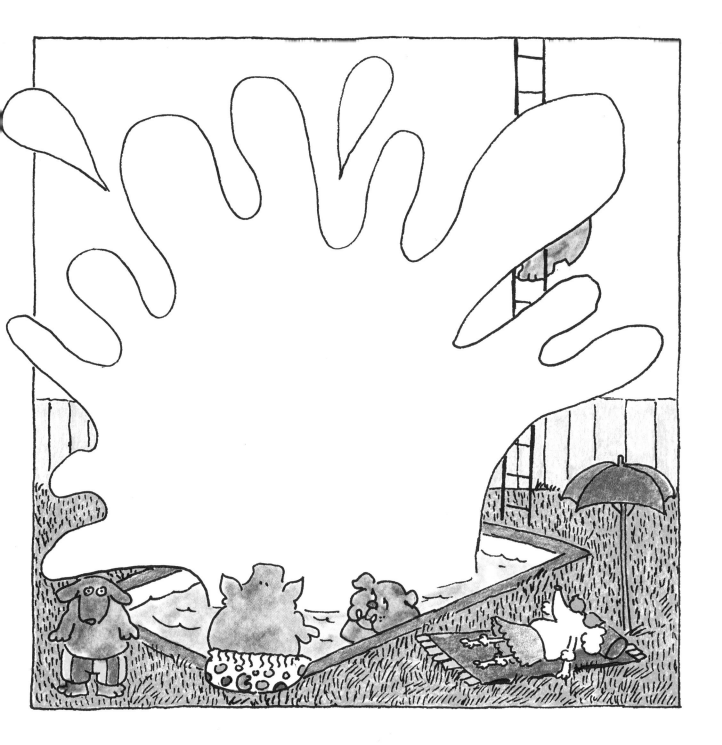

STORY NUMBER THREE

THE TRICK

George was fond of playing tricks on Martha.

But that was not Martha's idea of fun.

And when she found her house slippers

nailed to the floor, she was not amused.

Martha gave George the old

silent treatment.

"Oh no!" said George. "Not that!"

George decided to bake Martha's favorite cake.

"This will butter her up," he said.

When the cake was done,

George put it in a box.

And he went to look for a pretty ribbon.

"I have a surprise for you," said George.

"It's another trick!" said Martha.

"Not this time," said George.

"Then *you* open it," said Martha.

"Very well," said George. "I will."

Martha bit her nails, while George pulled off the ribbon.

Out jumped one rubber tarantula,

one stuffed snake, four plastic spiders,

and two real frogs!

"Egads!" cried George. "I've been tricked!"

"And by the way," said Martha.

"The cake was simply delicious."

STORY NUMBER FOUR

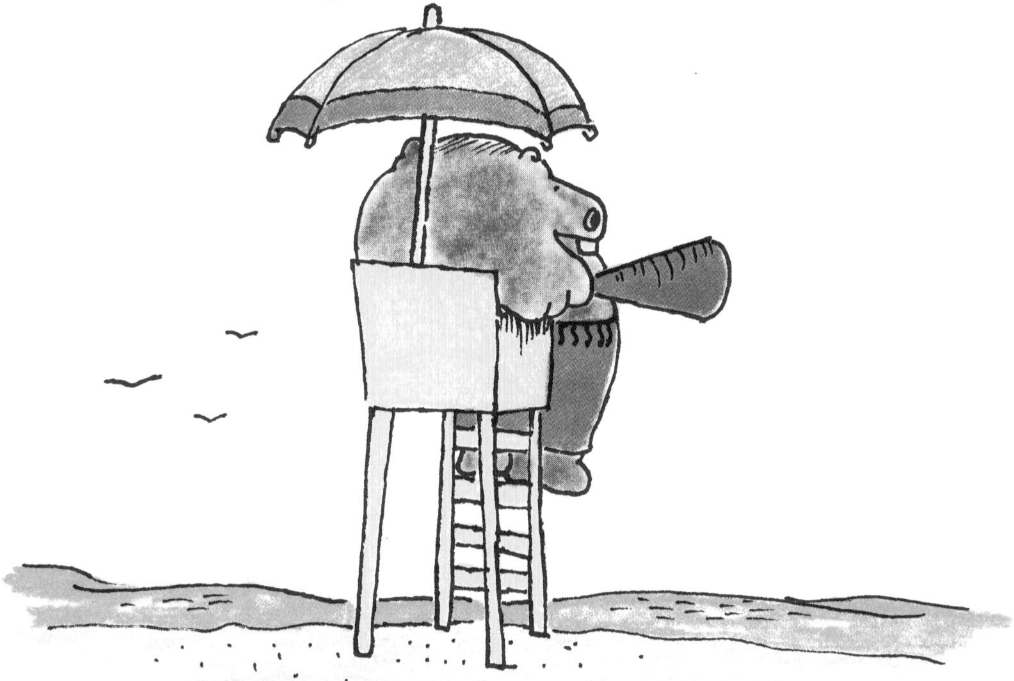

THE JOB

George was excited about his new job.

"It's hard work," said Martha.

"You must be *very* strict."

"I'll try," said George.

"No horsing around is allowed!"
said Martha.

"Thanks for the advice," said George.

"That's what friends are for,"
said Martha.

Very soon George saw that someone
was disobeying the rules.
"No horsing around!" he called through
his megaphone.
"It's all right!" shouted Martha.
"It's only me!"
"You heard me!" called out George.

George meant business.

And he gave Martha quite a bawling out.

"Well!" said Martha,

"And I thought we were friends!"

"Oh dear," said George. "Martha was right —
this *is* a hard job!"

George was all nice and cozy.

"May I join you?" said Martha.

"I'm reading," said George.

"I'll be as quiet as a mouse," said Martha.

"Thank you," said George.

And he went back to his book.

But soon Martha was fidgeting.

"Please!" said George.

"Have some consideration!"

"Sorry," said Martha.

George went back to his reading.

But in no time Martha was fidgeting again.

"That does it!" said George.

And he left.

At home he got all nice and cozy again.

He opened his book.

"It is important to be considerate
to our friends," said the book.

"It certainly *is!*" said George.

"Sometimes we are thoughtless without even
knowing it," said the book.

"*I'll* say!" said George.

"Martha should read this book."

He went to find her.

"I'm sorry I was fidgeting," said Martha.

"I got lonely."

"Oh," said George. "I never considered that."

"What did you want to tell me?" said Martha.

"Oh nothing," said George.

"I just got lonely too."

And they sat and told stories into the night.

Martha didn't fidget even once.